50 Soul Stirring Stories

50 Soul Stirring Stories

Prof. Shrikant Prasoon

Publishers
Pustak Mahal®

J-3/16 , Daryaganj, New Delhi-110002
☎ 23276539, 23272783, 23272784 • *Fax:* 011-23260518
E-mail: info@pustakmahal.com • *Website:* www.pustakmahal.com

Sales Centre

- 10-B, Netaji Subhash Marg, Daryaganj, New Delhi-110002
  ☎ 23268292, 23268293, 23279900 • *Fax:* 011-23280567
  E-mail: rapidexdelhi@indiatimes.com
- 6686, Khari Baoli, Delhi-110006
  ☎ 23944314, 23911979

Branches

Bengaluru: ☎ 080-22234025 • *Telefax:* 080-22240209
E-mail: pustak@airtelmail.in • pustak@sancharnet.in
Mumbai: ☎ 022-22010941, 022-22053387
E-mail: rapidex@bom5.vsnl.net.in
Patna: ☎ 0612-3294193 • *Telefax:* 0612-2302719
E-mail: rapidexptn@rediffmail.com
Hyderabad: *Telefax:* 040-24737290
E-mail: pustakmahalhyd@yahoo.co.in

ISBN 978-81-223-1273-7

Edition: 2012

Printed at : Param Offsetters, Okhla, New Delhi-110020

Dedicated

To All Human Beings:
Men and Women;
Old, Young and Children;

And to

My Dear Friend

Vijoy Kumar Sinha

Preface

A story, with many layers of meaning and possibilities of different interpretations; communicates its message in a roundabout, oblique manner, indirectly and yet in a familiar way; and clears dilemmas and bewildering situations.

It may convey spirituality or increase religiosity or provide moral support or enhance ethical values. In all, it gives immense pleasure and invaluable wisdom.

A true story is the food for reasoning and intellectual analysis with spirituality as its aim in the language of heart.

These marvelous and fabulous stories have been taken from Indian history, myths, culture, epics, dramas, folklore, fairy-tales, saints and from Buddha, Zen, Sufi, Sikh traditions; and also from European spirituality.

These are soul stirring tales. Each one will touch, smoothly and definitely the heart, mind and thus the soul. Powerful, positive, creative and effective moments have been depicted with bare minimum words and the details are left for the imagination and attitude of the individual reader to create and colour.

These short and delightful stories are designed to develop the mind, free it from distortions and connect with the inner spirit. They are truly inspiring and enlightening stories. They stir the soul and force the mind to think deeply in order to assimilate the ideas and meaning. The beauty, directness and simplicity of the messages get through to us one way or the other.

They deal mostly with – life in the present moment; its upheaval; continual distractions; different perspectives; overwhelming desires; deep attachment; strong resistance; unprejudiced judgments; instant delusions; mundane beliefs and transcendental thoughts as mental concepts and modifications.

They are well supported with meaningful illustrations in abstract art which are suggestive, ambiguous and non defined.

These stories are bound to enrich our minds and keep the path and vision lighted. So read them with an open mind, relate with them and assimilate the wisdom they impart.

Prof. Shrikant Prasoon
Opp. Town Police Station,
Motihari 845401
Chaparan East: Bihar, India
Mobile – 09868082133
Website: www.shrikantprasoon.com
E-mail: shrikantprasoon@yahoo.co.in
skprasoon@yahoo.com
info@shrikantprasoon.com

Contents

Prayers

Shānt-ākāram bhujag-shayanam padma-nābham suresham;

Vishwa-ādhāram gagan-sadrisham megha-varnam subhāngam.

Lakshmi-kāntam kamal-nayanam yogibhih-gyānag-gamyam;

Vande Vishnu bhava-bhaya-haram sarva-lokaika-nātham.

(He, whose whole form is the embodiment of peace; who sleeps on a python; a lotus has bloomed from whose navel; is the God of Gods; is the very basis of the Universe; is like the sky, handsome in appearance and of the cloud's colour; the spouse of Lakshmi; who takes away the worldly fears; that God is the master of all the Lokas.)

Shriyā shlishto vishnuh sthir-char-vapuh-veda-vishayo;

Dhiyām sākshi shuddho harih-asur-hantābja-nayan.

Gadi shankhi chakri vimal-vanmāli sthir-ruchih;

Sharanyo lokesho mam bhavatu krisno-akshi-vishayah.

(He, who is always seen with Lakshmi; is very attractive; the whole Universe is whose body; who is the subject of the Vedas; who is a witness to all knowledge and wisdom; is pure; has lotus eyes; who hold a conch, mace, wheel and wears a garland made of lotus flowers; has stable brightness and glow; and the saviour of all who seek shelter; that God of the Universe be before my eyes.)

1. Proper Lesson

A wealthy man requested an old scholar to cure his son of his bad habits.

The scholar took the youth for a stroll in a garden. Stopping suddenly, he asked the boy to pull out a tiny plant growing there. The youth held the plant between his thumb and forefinger and pulled it out.

The old man then asked him to pull out a slightly bigger plant. The youth pulled hard and the plant came out, roots and all.

"Now pull out that one," said the old man pointing towards a bush. The boy had to use all his strength to pull it out.

"Now take this one out," said the old man, indicating towards a guava tree. The youth grasped the trunk and tried to pull it out. But it refused to budge.

"I can't pull it out. It's impossible," said the boy, panting.

"So it is with bad habits," said the scholar "When they are saplings, they are tender and young, it is easy to pull them out but when they take hold they cannot be uprooted."

The boy soon realised what the old scholar was indicating at. He realised that he needed to get rid of his bad habits.

One session with the old scholar and one proper lesson changed the boy's life.

Soul Searching

There is perfection and imperfection everywhere and in everything. Focus on the action. Perform it wholeheartedly with sincerity and dedication and of course, wisdom. Success will follow. Work well done is joyous in itself. Action consecrated to a higher ideal is worship and spirituality evolves from it.

"Now pull out that one!"

2. Teaching Right and Wrong

When the Zen Master Bankei held his seclusion – weeks of meditation, pupils from many parts of Japan came to attend. During one of these gatherings, a pupil was caught stealing. The matter was reported to Bankei with the request that the culprit be expelled. Bankei however, ignored the case.

Later, the same pupil was caught in a similar act. It was reported but again Bankei disregarded the matter. This angered the other pupils, who drew up a petition asking for the expulsion of the thief. If otherwise, they would leave the gathering.

Bankei read the petition and smiled. He called everyone before him.

"You are wise brothers,'' he told them. "You know what is right and what is not right. You may go somewhere else to study if you wish, as you are wise. But this poor brother does not even know right from wrong. Who will teach him if I don't? I am going to keep him here even if all the rest of you leave."

There was complete silence. A torrent of tears cleansed the face of the pupil who was the thief. The desire to steal had vanished. He was a changed man.

Soul Searching

Punishment is not the only way to teach right and wrong or wholesome and unwholesome. Touch the weakness with soft and warm hands or sweet and suggestive words. It leaves more impact than punishment.

"I am going to keep him here even if all the rest of you leave."

3. Cycle of Evil

There was once a king who was so cruel and unjust that his subjects yearned for his death or dethronement.

However, one day he surprised them all by announcing that he had decided to turn over a new leaf.

"No more cruelty, no more injustice," he promised, and he was as good as his word. He came to be known as the 'Gentle Monarch'.

Months after his transformation, one of his ministers gathered enough courage to ask him what had brought about his change of heart. The king answered, "As I was galloping through my forests, I caught sight of a fox being chased by a dog. The fox escaped into its hole but not before the dog had bitten into its leg and lamed it for life. Later I rode into a village and saw the same dog there. It was barking at a man. Even as I watched, the man picked up a huge stone and flung it at the dog, breaking its leg. The man had not gone far when he was kicked by a horse. His knee was shattered and he fell to the ground, disabled for life. The horse began to run but it fell into a hole and broke its leg.

Reflecting on all that had happened, I thought: 'Evil begets evil. If I continue in my evil ways, I will surely be overtaken by evil.' So I decided to change."

The minister went away convinced that the time was ripe to overthrow the gentle king and seize his throne. Immersed in thought, he did not see the steps in front of him and fell, breaking his neck.

Soul Searching

Whether the cause is hidden or known, it will have its effect sooner or later. Righteous deeds are praised by all while unwholesome deeds are not liked, not even by the doer.

He did not see the steps in front of him and fell, breaking his neck.

4. No Escape: Taste Nectar Honey

One day, a man was going through a lonely place when an elephant started chasing him. He ran for safety. He found a dead well. He jumped into it to get rid of the elephant. But soon he saw snakes at the bottom. Oh! He clutched to a branch of banyan tree that had grown there. The elephant came there and lowered his trunk to catch the man. The man was beyond its reach.

The man was in a predicament: the snakes below and the elephant above. At that point of time, he saw that a black and a white rat were cutting the very branch that he was holding. A drop of honey fell on a leaf close to the man. He looked up and saw a big beehive. With his tongue, he tasted the honey. It was nectar, the nectar of life.

(In real life, the elephant a is day-to-day problem; man tries to take shelter in his cozy home but the danger of death in the form of snakes lurks there too. Moreover, the time is passing by swiftly as days and nights symbolised by white and black rats. When there is no escape, then one must face life to get Bliss and *Parmānad*, the absolute, eternal and immense pleasure symbolised by honey.)

Soul Searching

It is an undeniable fact that there is no escape from death. Then why should one worry about it. It will come at its appointed hour. In the meantime, instead of running away from life and its problems, one must live full, a complete life, doing only good and tasting the nectar, the honey which is the reward of righteous thought and deeds.

When there is no escape, then one must face life to get Bliss and *Parmānad*.

5. Headstrong Companion

Once upon a time there lived a *Bharunda*, a bird with two heads. One day, it found a strange fruit on the seashore. It picked it up and started eating it. The head that was eating the fruit, exclaimed, "Many a sweet fruits tossed by the sea have I eaten, but this beats them all! Is it the fruit of a sandalwood tree or that of the divine *pārijāta*?"

Hearing this, the other head asked to taste the fruit, but the first head refused, saying, "We have a common stomach, so there's no need for you to eat it too. I'll give it to our sweetheart, the *Bharundi*," and with that, it tossed the half-eaten fruit to the female.

From that day on, the second head carried a grudge against the first one and waited for an opportunity to take revenge. One day it found a poison fruit. Picking up the fruit, it said to the first head, "You selfish wretch! See, here's a poison fruit and I'm going to eat it!"

"Don't do that, you fool!" shrieked the first head, "You'll kill us both!" But the second head would not listen. It consumed the poison fruit, and soon the two-headed bird was dead.

Soul Searching

A man is known by the companion he keeps, as one is made or marred by the companion. Jealousy is one of the six great enemy of a men. The other five are sensuousness, anger, pride, attachment and lust. The saints advise to be away from these enemies and also from the persons that are dominated by these characteristics.

"See, here's a poison fruit and I'm going to eat it!"

6. Adjustment

The first Sikh Guru, Guru Nānak once went to Lahore. Although it was his first visit but he was well-known there. People knew him and adored him.

The established saints there did not like his arrival. They were afraid that he will steal the show from them. They sent a disciple with a bowl of milk filled up to the brim. The disciple said nothing and placed the bowl before Guru Nānak.

Guru Nānak read the message correctly. Symbolically, it showed that the place was already full of saints and there was no space for him.

Guru Nānak picked up a rose, plucked out a petal and silently and steadily placed it on the milk. The milk was not disturbed. He signalled the disciple to take the bowl back. He said nothing.

By doing so he sent an appropriate reply that he could adjust there without disturbing the established saints.

Soul Searching

Peaceful co-existence is the key to life on the earth. All the living beings have a right to be on the earth and pass their given days without disturbing others.

Guru Nānak picked up a rose, plucked out a petal and silently and steadily placed it on the milk.

7. Born, Ruled and Died

There was a king who wanted to know how other kings ruled and what great things they did that they were loved and respected by their subjects and made them immortal. In a few years, his learned historians and literateurs collected and brought a cart load of books before the king.

"Oh no! I can't read all these books. I don't have decades before me. Write it in short so that I may finish it." He lovingly looked at the books and said.

In a few years, the learned men brought fifteen volumes for him to read.

"Oh no! I can't read all these books. I don't have many years before me. Write it in short so that I may finish it." He longingly looked at the lovely leather-bound books.

In a few years, the learned men brought three volumes for him to read.

"Oh no! I have grown quite old. I can't read all these books. Write it in short so that I may finish it."

In a few years, the learned men brought the summary in one volume for the king to read. But he was on his death bed. His minister came to him with the book. He touched the book remorsefully and said, "Oh no! I can't read the book. It is my time for departure. Yet I want to know what they did. Please tell me in short."

"All the kings were born; they ruled and died," the minister said. But the king was not alive to listen to it.

Soul Searching

Perform as much righteous deeds as possible without waiting for auspicious time for time has its fixed, regular and incessant movement forward.

"Oh no! I can't read the book. It is my time for departure."

8. Be a Part of Delicious Cake

Just after returning from the school, a grandchild complained to his grandmother: "I won't go to school. My teachers reprimand me. My friends don't like me. They are better at study, in sports and in drawing artistic pictures. No one likes me. It is very bitter."

The grandmother said politely, "Don't say so much so fast all at once. You seem to be hungry for sweetness and angry for not getting love. I will give you cake to eat."

"Yes, I need it. I would love to eat one." The boy was jubilant. The grand mother gave him flour to eat. He ate it and his mouth was sour. He was harsher and bitter now with his complaint.

"Oh! It is tasteless. I can't eat it. Give me a cake."

The grandmother handed him a spoonful sugar and said, "It is sweet. You may enjoy it."

He put the mouthful sugar but could not relish it. "It's sweet but it's not tasty. Give me a cake." He was angrier.

The grandmother smiled at him and gave him butter with baking powder to eat. He filled up his hungry mouth again but he felt smoothing yet salty. He complained, "Oh grandma! What are you doing? I have lost my appetite. I can't eat these things."

"My son, these are the ingredients that make a delicious cake. Separately they are tasteless but when mixed together and baked well, they turn into a delicious cake. Why are you separate from friends and colleagues? Get mixed with them. Be a part of the group. You need love, so first give love. You want respect then show respect to them. We are not so wise, happy and honoured individually."

The boy kept on looking intently at the smiling face and brightened eyes of his grandmother. He was metamorphosed and no complaint came from him afterwards.

Soul Searching

Life is lovely and lovable when we mix together. It is bitter when separated.

Individually, we are not powerful because we don't share our strength, ability, love and sweetness. But in community, it is different. We are one with them and share unconditionally our strength, skill, ability, love, affection and respect.

We must join others with commitment which will transform us. We will not remain sugar or baking powder but change into delicious cake – tasty and full of vitamins.

It is the Yoga of wisdom. Love, respect and power is shared. Power of love is bliss but love for power is ego.

It is the Yoga of action. Love creates opportunities and initiates. It does not wait for introduction or order.

9. Giving Life Back

Ryokan was a Zen Master of repute. One day, a fisherman saw him walking towards the beach soon after a storm. The storm had washed up thousands of starfish on the shore and they were beginning to dry up. He knew, soon all of them would be dead and could not be received. Ryokan started picking up the starfishes and throwing them back into the sea.

The fisherman went up to the Master and said, "It is nice to try to give life back to a dying being. But I'm sure you cannot throw all these starfishes back into the sea? They will die in thousands here. I've seen it happen before. Your effort will make no difference."

"It will to this one," Ryokan said with confidence, throwing back another starfishes into the sea. He bent down to pick up yet another without looking at the fish that he had thrown into the sea.

The fisherman looked intently at him for some time and then, he started throwing the starfishes into the sea, faster than the Master. After some time, other fishermen also came and joined the work of giving life back to the dying starfishes. In that moment of crisis, they realised the true value of life and importance of right moment in life.

Soul Searching

Work diligently and righteously, as much for the self as for others today to make yesterday's dreams of happiness come true and to nurture tomorrow's visions of hope.

In that moment of crisis, they realised the true value of life.

10. Pride for What!

A king went to a saint for some spiritual lessons.

The saint asked, "O king! What will you do if you are dying of thirst and a person offers a bit dirty water for half your kingdom? Will you accept or deny?"

"Life is more important than the kingdom. I will give half of my kingdom and take the water." The king was honest and straightforward.

The saint asked again, "O king! What will you do if that dirty water gave rise to diseases; you are dying and a *Vaidya* offers cure for the other half of your kingdom? Will you accept or deny it?"

"Life is more important than the kingdom. I will give the other half of my kingdom and accept the medicine." The king affirmed again.

"O king! Then why are you proud of your kingdom which can be given away for dirty water and curative medicines?" the saint said.

Soul Searching

He who is engrossed in worldly pleasures cannot acquire supreme wisdom; and with pride one can't reach there. The absolute control over senses and ego is the process to gain knowledge and that will lead the knower to ultimate peace.

"Life is more important than the kingdom."

11. Theft of Wisdom

Anastasius was abbot of a monastery in Egypt. The monastery had a large collection of books, one among them being a rare volume worth a fortune. One day a visiting monk chanced upon the book and succumbing to temptation walked away with it. The theft was discovered the same day and it was not hard to guess who the culprit was but Anastasius refused to send anyone after the monk for fear that he might say he had not taken it and add the sin of perjury to that of theft.

The monk meanwhile was trying to sell the book and eventually found a buyer, a rich man who asked him to leave the book with him for a day so that he could get it evaluated.

When the monk had gone, the man hastened to the monastery and showed the book to Anastasius. The abbot recognised it instantly but did not say anything.

"A monk wants to sell it to me," said his visitor. "He's asking for a gold sovereign. You are knowledgeable about books. Is this book worth that much?"

"It's worth many times more than a sovereign," said the abbot. "It's a valuable book."

The man thanked the abbot and left. The next day when the monk came, he informed him that he would like to buy the book and was prepared to pay the price he had mentioned. The monk was overjoyed.

"Whom did you show it to?" he asked.

"I showed it to Anastasius, the abbot."

His visitor turned pale. "And what did he say?"

"He said the book was worth a sovereign."

"And what else?"

"He said nothing more."

The monk was both amazed and touched. He realised that the abbot had refused to reclaim his lost treasure so that he, the thief would not get into trouble. Nobody had ever shown him such love; nobody had ever behaved so nobly towards him.

"I've changed my mind, I don't want to sell it," he said and took the book from the man.

"When I learnt you had borrowed it, I decided to give it to you."

"I'll give you two sovereigns," said the customer.

The monk walked away without answering. He went directly to the monastery and handed the book to the abbot, tears brimming in his eyes.

"Keep it," said Anastasius. "When I learnt you had borrowed it, I decided to give it to you."

"Please take it back," pleaded the monk, "but let me stay here and attain wisdom from you."

His wish was granted. He spent the rest of his years in the monastery modeling his life after that of the saintly Anastasius.

Soul Searching

A wise person constantly lives in awareness of the basic unity of existence, free from the delusion of separateness. There is the unity of the spirit underlying the outer differences.

Grief and delusion come as a result of identification with the body, mind and intellect which are the little self. When one looks at the things from personal angle, there is sorrow. The moment one views the things from a larger perspective then wisdom and peace prevail.

12. Honour

Once, Alexander demoted one of his Generals. The General, now only a Commander of a small troop, did his work as usual.

It so happened that the Commander was to appear before Alexander. He looked at him with wonder and asked, "How is it that you are still very happy though demoted from the higher rank."

He answered, "Sir, I'm greatly pleased with my present position. Earlier, even the army officers were afraid of coming before me but now they meet me whenever they like. I solve their problems. They take my advice in all the matters. After demotion, I got the opportunity to serve them. They are pleased with me. It is my pleasure and its effect is my happiness."

"Don't you feel insult in demotion?" Alexander was apparently defeated.

"Where is honour – in post or in humanity?" he asked humbly. He continued, "There is pleasure, satisfaction and respect in serving others, not in unnecessarily punishing others."

Alexander showed his greatness by saying. "Don't take my mistake seriously. You are again promoted to the post of General."

Soul Searching

In current times, there might not be the equivalent of the great ones, who could unravel through example, the mystery of right or wrong; respect and disrespect; righteous or unrighteous; human or inhuman. So, before taking law in hand and punishing others, one must be prepared to face the karmic consequences of one's action.

13. Worldly Dharma

A young ascetic sitting in meditation under a tree was splattered by the droppings of a bird.

He looked up angrily at the culprit and such was the intensity of his wrath that the bird was reduced to ash.

His concentration disturbed, the ascetic got up and went in search of food. He knocked at the door of a house but there was no answer. He knocked again and the lady of the house shouted that she was coming. Later on, she came out with food and seeing that he was annoyed at having had to wait so long, smiled and said, "Please don't try to burn me with your angry glance like you did to that bird. My dharma as a housewife is first to take care of the needs of my family before attending to the needs of others."

The ascetic realised that she was no ordinary woman and was ashamed of himself. He asked her to teach him what dharma was. She said he should see Dharma Vyādha.

The ascetic went in search of Dharma Vyādha expecting to find a venerable sage but the man turned out to be a meat-seller.

Dharma Vyādha made him wait while he served his customers. When the ascetic showed signs of impatience, the meat-seller smiled and said, "Just as the woman's first duty was to her family, my first duty is to my customers."

So the ascetic waited. When the last of his customers had gone, the meat-seller turned to the ascetic and invited him home.

When they reached Dharma Vyādha's house, the ascetic was again made to wait while his host lovingly attended to his parents. It was quite some time before the meat-seller could return to his guest but the young man showed no trace of anger. A transformation had come over him.

"Now I know what dharma is," he said, rising and bowing to the meat-seller.

Giving up the path of asceticism, he returned home and begged forgiveness of his parents for having deserted them in their old age.

"I seek your blessings," he said, "to give me strength to do my dharma."

Soul Searching

We are all warriors in the battle of life. Each one of us has an obligation to perform. By performing all the worldly duties well, one can transcend delusion and move to higher state.

"Now I know what dharma is."

14. Ungovernable Temper

A Zen Master was delivering a lecture on self control. When the lecture was over and most of the students had returned, a new student came to him and said, "Master, I have an ungovernable temper. Help me get rid of it. It bothers me and others are affected too."

"You have something very strange," said the teacher. It is not healthy to possess an ungovernable temper or be possessed by one. Are you sure you have an ungovernable temper?"

"Yes Master," the student accepted candidly.

"Then, show it to me," the Master asked him again.

"Right now I cannot show it to you," the student said meekly.

"Why can't you?" the Master asked.

"It arises suddenly." The student volunteered the nature of his temper.

"When it arises suddenly at some instigation, incident or unknown entity, then it cannot be your own true nature," said the master, "if it were, you would be able to show it to me at any time. Why are you allowing something to trouble your life that is not yours?"

Thereafter, whenever the student felt his temper rising, he remembered the master's words and checked his anger. In time, he developed a calm and placid temperament.

Soul Searching

Tranquility can be maintained inside as insight is developed and attained with right approach and positive treatment.

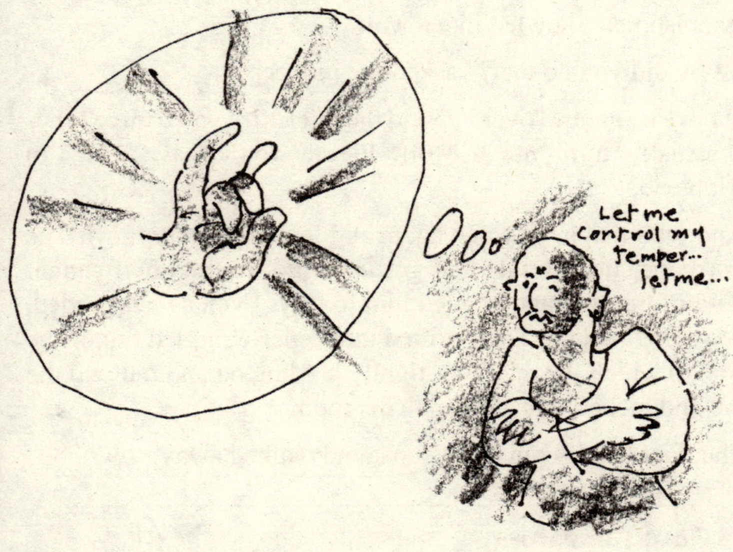

He remembered the master's words and checked his anger.

15. Crooked Howler

A thief hired a room at an inn and stayed there at night. The next morning, when he looked out of the window he saw the owner of the inn sitting in the courtyard. The man was wearing an expensive new coat which the thief decided would look good on his own body and give a reliable appearance.

He hatched a plan and accordingly went out. He sat by the side of the innkeeper, started up a conversation with him in a very casual manner. At first he yawned and then to the innkeeper's astonishment, howled like a wolf.

"Why did you do that?" asked the innkeeper.

"I have no control over it," said the thief. "If I yawn three times I actually turn into a wolf. Please don't leave me. I'm frightened!"

And with that he yawned again and let out another howl. The innkeeper turned pale and got up to go but the thief caught hold of his coat and begged him to stay. Even as he pleaded, he yawned again. The terrified innkeeper wriggled out of the coat to which the thief was tightly holding on and ran into the inn and locked himself inside his room.

The thief calmly put on the coat and walked away.

Soul Searching

There are numerous deception and innumerable deceptive persons. Hence, one should not believe every tale one hears.

The innkeeper ran into the inn and locked himself inside his room.

16. The Little Elephant

King Sheela Bhadra, of Bhāvapuri went into a dense forest named Chāmpakāranya, on a hunting expedition. Besides many other animals, he captured a gorgeous baby elephant. It was of noble breed. It appeared so cute and innocent that the king decided to keep it for personal use. His best *mahāut* was asked to train and take care of the little elephant.

After a fortnight, the baby elephant started showing haughty temper and naughty behaviour. The *mahāut* reported that in place of showing discipline, the elephant was becoming ill-mannered. The worried king ordered a minister to find out the cause and suggest ways to mend it.

The minister did not go directly to the baby elephant. He kept himself out of sight and climbed up a tree to watch the ill-mannered noble breed.

Early in the evening two ruffians came and sat under another tree quite close to the elephant. Two others joined them. Then half an hour later, three more joined them. They drank local wine, used unethical words, behaved badly, hurled abuses against each other and even against the persons that were not present there. It was their usual meeting place. The baby elephant was intently looking towards them.

The minister watched the proceedings for three nights. Then he submitted the report to the king. The king immediately stopped those ruffians. They were replaced by good men who were instructed to talk and behave well in a gentleman's way. There was a marked improvement in the behaviour of the baby elephant. Within a month, he started obeying the *mahāut*.

Soul Searching

We imitate others and if the other persons are ill-behaved then it precipitates emotions like anger, violence and attack. We are controlled by them.

Our moods and emotions swing. Slowly it becomes our second nature. Our temperament shows a perceptible change.

Life is unstable and unpredictable. None can guarantee to be always surrounded by good people and be in good mood.

The solution is then to be observant, watchful and alert, and avoid falling victim to the vagaries of the world.

When we are awake and watchful then we can boast of nurturing goodness, virtue, joy, love and be a human being in all aspects of life.

17. May be

Once upon a time, there was an old farmer who had worked hard in his fields and grown crops for many years. One day his horse ran away. Upon hearing the news, his neighbours came to give him solace.

"Such bad luck," they said sympathetically.

"May be," the farmer replied. He was non-committed and unaffected.

The next morning the horse returned, bringing with it two other wild horses. The neighbours came to congratulate, "How wonderful," the neighbours exclaimed.

"May be," replied the old farmer.

The following day, his only son tried to ride one of the untamed horses. He was thrown down and broke his leg. The neighbours again came to offer their sympathy on his misfortune.

"May be," answered the farmer.

The day after, military officials came to the village to draft young men into the army. Seeing that the son's leg was broken, they passed him by. The neighbours congratulated the farmer on how well things had turned out for him.

"May be," said the farmer. The events had no effect on him.

Soul Searching

Total identification with the events results in deep resentment or enthusiastic exultation but a balanced approach frees from remorse and ecstasy.

The insight shows that the meaning of incidents are not only what we perceive, it can be different, almost opposite.

18. Carrying Load in Mind

Two monks were returning to the monastery. It had rained and there were puddles of water on the road. At one place, a beautiful young woman was standing. Apparently she was waiting for someone who could help her. She was unable to walk across because of the muddy water. She requested them for help. The younger monk did not like the idea and stepped back in refusal. The elder monk went up to her, lifted her in his arms and left her on the other side of the road, and continued his way to the monastery. The younger monk accompanied him.

In the evening the younger monk came to the elder monk and said, "*Bhante*! As monks, we cannot touch a woman?"

The elder monk answered, "Touch for what?"

Then the younger monk explained, "*Bhante*! You lifted that woman on the roadside. Was it good to carry a woman in arms across the road?"

The elder monk smiled at him and said, "You are right but I left her on the other side of the road, while you are still carrying her."

Soul Searching

It is better to get rid of sensuous, unrighteous, unwholesome and impure feelings than to carry the load in mind.

19. Drum Beating

There was once a small boy who banged a drum all day and loved every moment of it. He would not be quiet, no matter what anyone else said or did. Six so-called Sufis were called in by the neighbours and asked to do something about the child.

The first so-called Sufi told the boy that he would, if he continued to make so much noise, perforate his eardrums. This reasoning was too advanced for the child, who was neither a scientist nor a scholar.

The second told him that drum beating was a sacred activity and should be carried out only on special occasions. It was of no avail because the child neither knew sacred occasions nor was interested in them.

The third so-called Sufi offered the neighbours plugs for their ears. They did not hear the drum now but they were unable to hear even the important messages.

The fourth gave the boy a book. But the boy had no interest in books.

The fifth gave some books to the neighbours that described a method of controlling anger through biofeedback. They could control their anger but the sound of drum disturbred their concentration.

The sixth and the last so-called Sufi gave the boy meditation exercises to make him placid and explained that all reality was imagination. The boy could not comprehend its meaning.

Eventually, a real Sufi came along. He looked at the situation, handed the boy a hammer and chisel, and said, "I wonder what is inside the drum?"

The boy was curious too. He took the hammer and chisel and broke open the drum. After that there was no drum beating.

Soul Searching

The mindset that we possess does not help us. It leads us to mediocre reality. Accept that reality is full of suffering and pain.

"I wonder what is inside the drum?"

20. Blind Man with a Lantern

Long ago, in Japan, a blind man started towards his friend's house. It was not very far but he blind men took a long time to reach there. He was welcomed by the family members of his friend and offered luncheon. After an hour or so, his friend returned. They talked for many hours.

During that time in Japan, bamboo-and-paper lanterns were used with candles inside. The blind man, while returning during night, was offered such a lantern to carry home with him.

"I do not need a lantern," he said. "Darkness or light is all the same to me. A lantern will be a problem and a burden."

"I know you do not need a lantern to find your way," his friend replied, "but if you don't have one, someone else may run into you. He may hit you hard and you may fall down and get injured. So, you must take it."

The blind man started off with the lantern and before he had walked very far someone ran squarely into him.

"Look out where you are going!" he exclaimed to the stranger. "Can't you see this lantern?"

"Your candle has burnt out, brother," replied the stranger. "Don't you know?"

There was no reply.

Soul Searching

The mind receives the signals of light, movement, sound and silence. Synchronise the mind with physical movement to make up for other deficiencies. With glowing inner light, no outer aid will be needed.

"Your candle has burnt out, brother," replied the stranger.

21. Winners or Losers

Once, the Gods announced a race for all the animals. Besides many consolation boons, the winner was to get the desired boon. The *tithi*, *pala* and *sthān* (the date, month and time) were fixed and all animals were asked to practice and participate. The demigods and *gandharvas* were appointed as volunteers to keep watch on everything.

The animals not only started to practice but they also began to discuss what they would ask as boon, as each animal wanted to be the winner.

The smaller animals were in a predicament. How would they compete against the larger animals with longer legs and higher pace. Each animal thought of at least one advantage over the others. But they could come up with several disadvantages, as they thought of all the other animals with different physique and power.

The frogs found themselves to be the most miserable as they could only jump and the problem was the distance and time. They were neither in a position to take longer jumps repeatedly for longer duration nor cover longer distances all alone. They held a meeting every day for a week. On the last day, their coach declared that the frogs will definitely win the race and the boon they for would ask for would be high sound. Everyone agreed on the boon though they did not believe in his declaration of a guaranteed win. Yet, the coach was given ample power and free hand.

In place of one participant, the coach selected 150 participants of similar size, weight and appearance. He trained them apart as in a relay race. The one ahead was to remain at the side of the road. The frog coming from behind was to jump towards the next one and from there on the next one was to start jumping.

On the scheduled time, date and place, the race began. It was a unique race never thought or heard of. All the vacant spaces along the sides of the straight track were filled up by large number of animals as spectators.

The frogs synchronised their jumps and participated so well that they won the race. At the award ceremony, the boon so desired was asked and revealed as higher speaking sound. The chief guest said, "Ok." But a *gandharva* soon reached at the spot and stopped him. He had caught the frogs playing

The frogs synchronised their jumps and participated so well that they won the race.

the trick. He informed everyone how the frogs had cheated the other animals. The chief guest said that he had already accepted their demand and it was too late to reverse the boon. No sooner a God suggested that he was empowered for additions and subtractions. He then got an idea and made changes in his announcement: "OK, you will get higher sound but since you hid at different places and were in the race and out of it also, so you will live on the land and in the water and your sound will increase only during the rainy season. During other seasons, you will remain hidden away from others.

On hearing the announcement, frogs could not decide whether they were winners or losers.

Soul Searching

Life is always a competition: a race or a test. Both truthfulness and deception are ways to win but apparent winners are often seen to be great losers and apparent losers have come out as winners. Strange are the ways and results. The accumulated happiness and desired boon at the finish, the end of life count not the lead in the half way mark. The soul stirs at unseen grief and unsaid pain.

It pays to be 'one' and 'united' and 'fair'.

22. Skill and Control

After winning several archery contests, the young and boastful champion challenged a Zen Master who was renowned for his skill as an archer. The young man demonstrated remarkable technical proficiency when he hit a distant bull's eye on his first try, and then split that arrow with his second shot.

"There," he said to the old man, "see if you can match that!"

Undisturbed, the Master did not draw his bow, but rather motioned for the young archer to follow him up to the mountain. Curious about the old fellow's intentions, the champion followed him high to the mountain until they reached a deep chasm spanned by a rather flimsy and shaky log. Calmly stepping on and walking up to the middle of the unsteady and certainly perilous temporary bridge, the old Master picked a far away tree as a target, drew his bow and arrow, and shot a clean, direct hit.

"Now it is your turn," he said as he gracefully stepped back on to the safe ground.

Staring with terror into the seemingly bottomless water body and beckoning abyss, the young man could not dare to step out on to the shaking log. He had no desire to shoot at a target.

"You have much skill with your bow," the Master said, knowing his challenger's predicament, "but you have little skill with the mind that lets loose the shot."

Soul Searching

Control over hand and target can be achieved with some control over mind but complete control over mind is required for balance and balanced growth.

23. Three Dolls

A sage presented a prince with a set of three small dolls. The prince was not amused.

"Am I a girl that you give me dolls?" he asked.

"This is a gift for a future king," said the sage. "If you look carefully, you'll see a hole in the ear of each doll."

"So what?"

The sage handed him a piece of string.

"Pass it through each doll," he said.

Intrigued, the prince picked up the first doll and put the string into the ear.

It came out from the other ear.

"This is one type of person," said the man. "Whatever you tell him, comes out from the other ear. He doesn't retain anything."

The prince put the string into the second doll. It came out from the mouth.

"This is the second type of person," said the sage. "Whatever you tell him, he tells everybody else."

The prince picked up the third doll and repeated the process. The string did not reappear from anywhere else.

"This is the third type of person," said the sage. "Whatever you tell him is locked up within him. It never comes out."

"Who is the best type of person?" asked the prince.

The man handed him a fourth doll, in answer.

When the prince put the string into the doll, it came out from the other ear.

"Do it again," said the sage.

The prince repeated the process. This time the string came out from the mouth. When he put the string a third time, it did not come out at all.

"This is the best type of person," said the sage. "To be trustworthy, a man must know when not to listen, when to remain silent and when to speak out."

Soul Searching

The balance in feeling, thinking, doing or in anything is the best thing. The only thing difficult is to know the balancing point of both matter and spirit.

24. Friendly with or against Time and Tide

On a tree inclined towards a river, there was a dry thin branch. It was forked. At the forked end, it was divided in two in semicircular shape. Though dried up, they had a bit of life left.

One day, the smaller among them, said, "I'm ready to fall. I can fall anytime. The branch will not hold us."

The other was angry and said, "Why will he not hold us? We have come out of it. We can force it to hold us."

But a westerly breezy wind came there singing, and speeded up near that forked branch and passed away. The force, though not very hard yet was enough to break the branch from the joint and separate the two semicircular dried up woods – thin and weightless.

Both of them fell into the flooded river whose fast currents were playing havoc. The smaller one felt the coolness and swiftness, and realised that the swings on currents will provide great pleasure. It smiled when it rose up and tried to catch water when it fell fast and was submerged in deep water for some unknown period of time. It flowed and covered a long distance as if it was relaxing on a wet bed.

It reached to a turning and was held there. It was a very exciting and adventurous journey for the small dried up branch.

The other one did not like the separation. It tried to disobey the breeze but fell into the river. It knew wetness. It had played during rains but the currents were different and tumultuous and misbehaved. It was angry. It tried to beat the water by jumping high and falling fast because it was being repeatedly beaten by the unruly currents. It fought bravely and resisted with all its might and intelligence, but every time it tried to oppose it was beaten hard. Soon fatigue overtook it. It wept but the currents were forcing their way ahead and were not in a mood to wait and see who was weeping and why.

A westerly breezy wind came there singing, and speeded up near that forked branch and passed away.

At last, it reached the same turning. It was held there. It was tired, defeated and weeping. The small branch came close to the latecomer to soothe the feelings but said nothing, although it wanted to say a lot. The wounded branch also wanted to say a lot but was not feeling like telling the true feelings. It also did not say anything but wished to be closer to the first one and liked it.

Soul Searching

When there was nothing, there was time. After the creation, energy, force, opposition, birth, death and infinite number of subtle and material forms came into existence. Time rules over all.

Those who are friendly to time or surrender to it, get immense pleasure and bliss. Those who defy it, oppose it are wounded in numerous ways and at many places before falling into the final sleep.

27. Wealthy, Warrior King

A king built his great empire by conquering kings, places and by killing people. He had accrued treasures from all over the world. Now, he was old. He asked, "Everything that I have amassed must be displayed for me and others to see."

When everything was ready, he came to see them. For several hours, he looked at gold ornaments and coins; precious stones and jewels; diamond-studded crowns and other priceless objects.

Suddenly, he began to cry. He told his courtiers, "Throughout my warriors-days, I kept on killing people. I have slain tens of thousands of people, causing thousands of women widowed and children orphaned for these precious objects. In the process I lost my soul. Yet, not even the smallest piece of gold can go with me now that I'm about to die.

So, now I order you, when you take my body to the burial place extend both my empty hands outside the coffin. I wish to let people know that with all my wealth, I left the world empty-handed. No material wealth can go with the dead.

Soul Searching

The state of no mind come when one is truly humble and has no ignorance and no knowledge; when there is neither a question nor the need of an answer.

28. Overstuffed and Overflowing

A University Professor went to meet a Zen Master. The Zen Master welcomed the Professor and gave him a seat. The Professor introduced himself. While doing so, he used some adjectives that clearly smelt of his ego. Then he casually mentioned the cause behind his visit. He wished to learn Zen philosophy and practice Zen Meditation.

Someone brought tea for them. The Zen Master had heard all but said nothing till now. He pulled the tray closer and started preparing tea. He started pouring tea into the visitor's cup. The cup was full to the brim yet the master kept on pouring tea into the cup. The tea started overflowing.

The Professor watched with amazement. But he could not control himself. He impatiently said, "O Master! The cup is overstuffed and overflowing. It will not take more."

"You are also like the cup – overstuffed and overflowing. You too can't absorb any more," the Master said patiently.

The Professor said nothing but kept looking at the Zen Master.

Soul Searching

First empty the self from the preconceived ideas. Get rid of your prejudices to understand the nature of things, beings and the Universe.

"O Master! The cup is overstuffed and overflowing."

29. Filling Sieve with Water

A sage had given a discourse on creative thinking. Afterwards his disciples approached him and asked him to set them a problem that required them to think creatively. The sage gave them a sieve and asked them to fill it with water at the sea, nearby. They were gone for a long time. Finally, he went down to the beach to see what they were doing, and found them seated morosely around the sieve.

They scrambled to their feet when they saw him.

"You've set us an impossible task, sir," said the oldest of the disciples. "It's just not possible to fill a sieve with water."

"Are you sure?" asked the sage, picking up the sieve. "Sometimes it helps to step back and view the problem from a different angle."

He waded into the water and threw the sieve far out into the sea. It sank.

"There!" said the sage. "It's full of water now."

Soul Searching

Emptying the mind by throwing out the rubbish and all negative thinking or filling up the mind with positive spiritual ideas and aspirations needs an effort out of the ordinary.

He waded into the water and threw the sieve far out into the sea.

30. Sinner vs Virtuous

A woman was brought before the Christ followed by a large crowd. Her hands were tied behind. Her head was bent low. She was charged with illicit relations and the crowd was asking for her to be beheaded.

"There is no doubt that the woman is a sinner. She is not denying the charge. So, you can do whatever you like. All the persons are allowed to hit her with five stones each." Christ said without any expression of emotion, compassion or kindness.

The woman shuddered. She had the hope that Christ, the Saviour, will save her but he had announced the severest punishment. The people were ready with stones in hands.

She heard the loud sound of Christ, "But the first stone is to be hit by the person who is completely pious; who has never committed a sin in life. If a sinner hits her first, then he will get the same punishment."

The hands raised high, came down. The woman looked towards Christ with tearful eyes. But he himself was looking towards the crowd and continuously encouraged them to hit the woman hard, "She is a sinner. She must be punished but only by the pious and the virtuous."

The crowd started receding. After some time, only the woman and Christ remained there. He went to the lady, untied her hands and said, "You are free. You can go anywhere you like. God is merciful. He forgives his children. Pray God to forgive you."

Soul Searching

Equality is a spiritual concept, for all of us are spiritually equal. But we need to be careful to port this concept on to the material plane of dispensing justice.

"The first stone is to be hit by the person who is completely pious; who has never committed a sin in life."

31. Medicine after Death

There was a very devotee lady who was the daughter of religious parents. She was married to a business tycoon. His husband knew nothing but money. She always advised him to devote some time for charitable deeds and in worshipping the God. Every time he replied, "What is the hurry? There is a lot of time."

Once, he fell ill. The wife was looking after him. The doctor gave him medicines. The wife kept the medicine on one side. The husband waited for it. Then asked, "Give me the medicine."

She replied, "What is the hurry? There is a lot of time."

He was angry, "Will I take the medicine after death?"

She said confidently, "Will you worship after death? Who knows when will the death strike?"

He looked at the determined face of his wife. Then he smiled. From the next day, he started worshipping and doing charity.

Soul Searching

We have no control over the past and the future is unknown. It is the present when we are alive and energetic. Whatever we have to do can be done in the present, either now or never.

"Will I take the medicine after death?"

32. Prospect

Once, the ass of a washerman and the ass of a magician met in the small park in a rich residential colony. They had been enjoying the soft Italian grass in the drain like cricket pitch. They saw each other happily and affectionately touch the neck of each other.

Then the customary introduction was performed. The ass of the washerman said:

"I work with a very busy washerman. He is mostly busy in washing and collecting clothes and in returning the ironed clothes to the customers and collecting money in lieu thereof. Occasionally, he would place a not so heavy weight on me and I had to carry it to the drying river. Rest of the time, I'm free to enjoy the greenery in all the three small parks in the vicinity. He was never in danger as he was not allowed to go to the crowded main road."

Oh! It is not a good thing to show one's art before the rowdy, unintelligent crowd. It is no life at all to keep on moving from one residential area to another wandering, showing playfulness for money. My master also works for money but the known person of our residential area come and pay with honour. It is the wages of our hard labour.'

The ass of the magician showed mixed reaction: "Oh! You're intelligent. Whatever you are telling is true! I like your statement! I'm pleased! But you don't know the high prospect in my job."

"What is the high prospect?" He showed his eagerness to know it.

"My master has a very beautiful and shapely daughter. She is the life of our group. She moves on a tight rope some seven feet high in the sky. She is an expert and crosses the rope from one end to another then turns and returns back."

"But what is the prospect in it?" He was not interested in rope walking.

The ass of the magician continued: "At the start of every walk on the rope when she is up on the rope and try to steady her attractive body and small staff, the magician makes an announcement – if you walk up to the other end and come

"But you don't know the high prospect in my job."

back to this side again, I'll marry you to a prince but if you fail and fall on the way, then I'll marry you to this very ass. He clearly indicates towards me. I'm sure, someday, my lucky day the beautiful dame would fall and get married to me. This is the high prospect!"

Soul Searching

Imaginary and dreamy prospect! The expectations of unexpected wealth, luxurious living and sensual pleasure force one to be satisfied in the unhealthy and unhygienic condition and not to try for a concrete shift. Such men hardly do anything to grow from inside and do something concrete . They remain at the end almost the same what they were at the beginning.

33. Anger

A king was fond of birds. In his personal garden he had thousands of different birds but a partridge was his favourite. It played with the king. It would sit on his shoulders and accompany the king almost everywhere.

Once, he went for hunting. His horse galloped faster and he went ahead of his hunting group. In the forest, the king lost his way. He was thirsty. He searched for water. From the joint of stones he saw water falling drop by drop. He made a bowl of leaves and placed under it. After some time, it filled up but when the king picked it up for drinking, the partridge hit it hard, and the water fell. The thirsty king became angry.

He again placed the leafy bowl and again it filled up in a few minutes. But when the king picked it up for drinking, the partridge again hit it hard and the water fell down. The angry king caught the bird and twisted its neck so hard that the bird died.

Just out of curiosity, he looked up. There was a dead snake at the joint of the stones.

"Oh! The bird tried to save me from the poisonous water and I killed it foolishly." The king repented but a little too late.

Soul Searching

He is a fool who fails to control his anger. He gets its punishment and repents later like the king who killed the bird:

Krodho utapattau hi krodhasya phalam guhyāti moodha dhih;
Sa shochati tu kim pashchāt pakshi- ghātaka bhupavat.

34. Biting is Prohibited not Hissing

A seer was passing through a village when he heard the weeping of many men and women in a chorus. He stopped and enquired. The villagers said that there was a cobra in the hole of the banyan tree. He had a habit of biting someone after every few months. No one ever survived. This time he has bitten the only child of a very gentle farmer. Though the farmer is not weeping but most of the villagers are weeping for the growing child.

The seer went straight to the crowd and looked at the child. Foam was oozing out of his mouth. He was almost senseless and was about to die. The seer came into action. He took out some herbs from his carry bag and administered the child. He cut open the biting place and rubbed the herbs. After a few hours, the boy regained his senses. He administered more herbs and the boy was out of danger.

The seer then went straight to the hole shown by the people. He called the cobra out. The cobra obeyed. He then said, "From now on don't bite any one."

The seer went away. The villagers were happy.

The seer was returning through that very village after two months when he saw many children throwing stones at something. He stopped and enquired. Someone who did not recognise him informed that a saint once ordered the dangerous cobra not to bite anyone. He obeys. But some unruly children now and then throw stones on it. He is wounded and in a state of dying.

The seer straightway went to the snake tearing off the children and asked, "Why are you in such a state?"

The cobra could hardly utter, "It was you who admonished me from biting anyone and are asking me why I'm in such a state."

The seer said in the same vein, "O fool! I had admonished you from biting but not from hissing. It is your duty to save yourself."

The cobra understood. With pain all over the body, he raised his hood as high as he could and hissed at his wounded best. The children ran away helter and skelter as fast as they could. It gave a message to the villagers that the kind seer has again given order to the cobra to bite anyone who throws stones on him.

"I had admonished you from biting but not from hissing."

Soul Searching

It is a sin and a crime to be destructive or to bring harm to anybody which results in the loss of life or property. But it is the pious duty of every living creature to save one's life by applying whatever power one possesses, and of course by ethical means.

What is important in life? People usually answer that wealth or house or wife or son is important in life. No. It is gross error. The only thing important in life is life. If one has no life then what is the use of the wealth or house? If one has no life then his own relatives and neighbours will put him on pyre to burn or place in the grave.

35. On the Roof

One summer noon when the sun was too hot to bear, the son of a farmer was repairing the roof of his hut. The farmer was anxious. He asked him to come down and try to finish the work in the afternoon or tomorrow. The monsoon was about a month away. The son did not listen to his father. He said, "It is just a work of fifteen minutes more. Then I will come down."

The farmer was tensed. He waited for fifteen minutes but the son showed no sign of descending from the roof. The farmer asked him in angry tone, "Come down immediately or I will take some drastic step."

The son laughed, "Don't be angry. I will finish it soon and come down."

The farmer entered the house and came out with his one-year-old grandson. He put him on the hut roof while holding him with both hands. The son saw and cried, "What are you doing. The sun is very hot. He will get a sun stroke. Take him inside."

The farmer said plainly, "Why? Your son will get sun-stroke and the sunrays will spare my son."

The farmer's son immediately came down, took his son and went inside.

Soul Searching

One realises the love, anxiety and suffering of parents when one attains parenthood. God is eternal parent as *Prakriti* and *Purush* or *Ardhanārishwar* and loves, cares and is anxious. He gives an opportunity to grow stronger from inside so that one enters into him for eternal union and for metamorphosis and *Nirvāna*.

36. The Palace : An Inn

Once, a saintly person came to Abou ben Adham, the king of Balkha

Abou asked, "What do you want?"

The stranger said placidly, "I want nothing. I wish to stop in this inn only for a night."

Abou showed surprise, "It is not an inn. It is my palace."

The stranger asked, "Who owned and lived in it before you?"

Abou's answer was simple, "My father owned it and lived here."

The stranger asked, "Who owned and lived in it before him?"

Abou's answer was again simple, "My grandfather owned it and lived here."

The stranger asked, "Who owned and lived in it before him?"

Abou's answer was simple, "My great grandfather owned it and lived here."

The stranger asked, "Who owned and lived in it before him?"

Abou's answer was similar, "His father lived here who got it constructed."

The stranger had another question, "Where have all these owners who lived here departed?

Abou was not very confident with his correct answer, "They are all dead."

The stranger asked sweetly, "Then, is it not an inn in which, people stay and after some time depart?"

This conversation changed Abou ben Adham. He had no interest left in worldly possessions. He accepted the world as transitory. Now, for him, it was more important to find the soul and God.

Soul Searching

The greedy people get nothing. A humble man gets many times more, and more valuable things in the form of insight, tranquility, solace, peace, health and happiness.

37. Extreme Patience and Tolerance

One day dacoits abducted the son of a rich businessman and sold him to a cruel trader. The trader forced the boy to work hard and gave him little to eat. He would also often beat the boy. One day another businessman came there and recognised the boy.

He sympathised with the boy and said, "Here you must be in a lot of pain and suffering."

"Why to worry about that state which is not to last long in this ever-changing world?" the boy answered placidly.

Many years passed. The trader grew old and died leaving behind a wife and a minor son. The boy was now young and free as the trader freed him while dying. Since the boy was earning he looked after the wife and son of the trader.

The same businessman happened to visit them again. He met the young man and asked, "How are you now?"

"Why to worry about that state which is not to last long in this ever-changing world?" the young man said very calmly.

Many years passed, the young man made enough progress to be declared the Chief of the place. The son of the trader was with him, however, his mother passed away.

The same businessman met him after a few years and congratulated him for his wealth and position. The young man expressed the same opinion, yet again, "Why to worry about that state which is not to last long in this ever-changing world?" he answered placidly.

Time passed, he now became the king of that country. The same businessman, who was now old, learnt it and somehow managed to meet him. He congratulated and offered gifts and expressed his satisfaction and pleasure, "It is really a pleasure to see a man coming to the top from the bottom."

The king thanked him and repeated his statement: "Why to worry about that state which is not to last long in this ever-changing world. Why to be aggrieved or elated?"

Soul Searching

It is the faith in the God and the self and the knowledge of the world that gives immense capacity to make steady progress as the positive qualities are enhanced rather multiply. By following a simple path one becomes extraordinary; a being of profound cosmic subtlety.

38. Deeds and Misdeeds

A certain man had laid his net across the river; having laid his net, he killed a quantity of fish. Meanwhile, there came a raven, and perched beside him. It looked hungry and seemed to be greatly interested in the fish. It was much to be pitied. So the fisherman washed one of the fish, and threw it to the raven. The raven ate the fish with great joy. Afterwards the raven came again. Though it was a raven, it spoke thus, just like a human being, "I am very grateful for having been fed on fish by you. If you will come with me to my old father, he too will thank you. So you had better come."

The man went with the raven. Being a raven, it flew through the air. The man followed it on foot. After they had gone a long way, they came to a large house. When they got there, the raven went into the house. The man also went in. When he looked, it appeared like a human being in form, though it was a raven. There were also a divine old man and a divine old woman besides the divine girl.

The girl was the raven who had led the man to that house. The divine old man spoke thus, "I am very grateful to you. As I am very grateful to you for feeding my daughter with good fish, I have had you brought here in order to reward you."

Then there were a gold puppy and a silver puppy. Both these puppies were given to the man. The divine old man spoke thus, "Though I should give you treasures, it would be useless. But if I give you these puppies, you will be greatly benefited. As for the excrements of these two puppies, the gold puppy excretes gold and the silver puppy excretes silver. This being so, you will be greatly enriched if you sell these excrements to the officials. Understand this!"

Then the man, with respectful salutations went away carrying with him the two puppies, and came to his own house. Then he gave the puppies a little food at a time. When the gold puppy excreted, it excreted gold for him. When the silver puppy excreted, it excreted silver for him. The man greatly enriched himself by selling the metal.

Thereupon another man, for the sake of imitation, set his net in the river. He killed a quantity of fish. Then the raven came. The man smeared a fish with mud, and then threw it to the

So the fisherman washed one of the fish, and threw it to the raven.

raven. The raven flew away with it. The man went after it, and at last, after going a long way, reached a large house. He went in there. The divine old man was very angry. He spoke thus, "You are a man with a very bad heart. When you gave my daughter a fish, you gave it smeared all over with mud. I am very angry. Still, though I am angry, I will give you some puppies, as you have come to my house. If you treat them properly, you will be benefited." Thus spoke the divine old man, and gave a gold puppy and a silver puppy to the man. With a bow, the man went home with them.

The man thought thus, "If I feed the puppies plentifully, they will excrete plenty of metal. It would be foolish to have them excreting only a little at a time. So I will do that, and become very rich." Thinking thus, he fed the puppies plentifully on anything, even on dirty things. Then they excreted no metal for him. They only excreted dirty dung. The man's house was full of nothing but dirty dung.

As for the former man, who had received puppies from the divine old man, he fed them on nothing but good food, a little aı a time. Gradually, they excreted metal for him. He was greatly enriched.

As for bad-hearted man, the Gods became angry at his various misdeeds. It was for this reason that, on account of their anger, even a gold puppy excreted nothing but dung.

Soul Searching

In ancient times, with regard to men who wished to grow rich they could grow rich if their hearts were as good as possible. It is the good deeds that give gold and silver. The bad deeds change the gold and silver into dung.

39. Final Lesson

A prince had just completed his education. On the day of convocation, the king and the courtiers also came. When the convocation address was over, the prince came to his Guru for final obeisance. He touched the feet of his Guru. The Guru said, "Bring me a stick."

The prince brought a stick. The Guru took it and without any provocation hit the prince hard twice with the stick and then gave the blessings: *Jivet Basantah Shatam Prasannamanāh!*

No one heard the blessing. All the persons present there were astonished at the sight of the beating. They were wondering why it happened when the prince had done nothing wrong. The humble prince stood silently before the Guru.

"Now, you can go with your father," the Guru ordered.

But the king had a question, "O Learned Guru! May I ask why did you beat the prince and why did you select this very moment for his beating?"

The Guru said, "This was the last lesson. Your son is so humble that I did not get an opportunity to punish him. So, I chose this moment to punish him in the presence of all. It would not have been so effective had I given it earlier. O king! Your son is brave, wise and humble but he has to rule the people. He must know the pain of punishment, otherwise he may not be able to do justice. He must experience the pain."

The king saluted the Guru, the courtiers followed suit. Then, they returned back along with the prince.

Soul Searching

To enjoy pleasant days is one thing and to experience pain and suffering is quite another. It opens the inner eyes and tests resistance and sustenance. It gives wisdom too.

40. Inspired Performance

One day a writer was going through a street. He saw a labourer who was hammering and crushing stones into chips. He was murmuring something in an unpleasant tone. He could not make out what his utterances were but through the tone it was clear that he was expressing his anguish. Before he could pass him on, he heard the whistling sound of a pleasant tune. He turned towards it and saw another labourer that hurried up to the stone-chips. He kept on whistling the pleasant tune, threw his iron cauldron down, filled it up with the chips, lifted it up and placed on his head and returned back. The writer was amazed. He could not move away. He stood there for some time and watched them. The same process continued.

Out of curiosity, the writer walked up to the first labourer and asked, "What are you doing?"

"Don't you see I'm crushing my fate?" promptly came a harsh reply. He stepped back.

When the other labourer came whistling another nice tune, he asked the same question, "What are you doing?"

"Don't you see I'm constructing a temple?" He promptly gave a confident and enthusiastic reply. That is the highest kind of spirit and most inspired performance. The difference in the approach of both the workers was obvious.

Soul Searching

An inspired performance can come to the fore only when a person possesses such enthusiastic, confident and spirited approach, nature and character. One thing is sure, inspired workers are more productive. They show greater skill and accuracy. The higher and greater the level of inspiration, the more will be the output of the workforce. Disgruntled workers fail to complete the task, and have an alibi for everything. One needs ethics, design and security. Only then one can perform in an inspired way and feel the pleasure, rather a blissful state after every inspired performance.

Out of curiosity, the writer walked up to the first labourer and asked, "What are you doing?"

41. Gratification through others' Satisfaction

Once, a very learned philosopher fell ill. His condition kept on deteriorating. When many physicians failed then came a reputed physician.

He examined him and declared, "The patient should not be given a single drop of water till I re-examined him. He may die if water is given."

The people looking after him became careful and ensured that no water was given to the patient. His thirst grew. He was apprised of the doctor's instructions. When his thirst became unbearable, he thought over the problem and came up with a solution.

He called his wife and said, "Invite the Brāhmins and give them sorbet, melon water and coconut water to drink in my presence."

It was obeyed and arranged. While they were drinking sorbet and fruit water, the philosopher was looking at them gregariously. He was losing the intensity of his thirst. Later on he felt no thirst.

He smiled and said, "I drank it with them."

Soul Searching

A person should see and treat other creatures as a replica of his own self. Then he is wise and then there is no pain:

Ātmavat sarva bhuteshu yah pashyati sah panditāh.

"I drank it with them."

42. Search for an Honest Man

A king needed an honest man. His employees were collecting taxes and filling their own pockets without depositing it in the treasury. He discussed the problem with his wise minister. The minister suggested, "Get it announced throughout the kingdom that you need an honest man; fix a date of interview and when the candidates come before you, ask them to dance."

The king could not see the relation between dance and an honest man but he had ample faith in his minister. The announcement was made with due urgency.

The news spread like wild fire and many candidates came. They were asked to pass through a dark passage in order to reach the king. They gathered before the king who asked them to dance.

They were shy of dancing and stepped back. However, one person started dancing but he did not know how to dance. The king smiled at his dance which had no rhythm.

The minister said to the king, "He is the only honest man among them."

"How is it?" The king wanted to know.

"In the dark passage, at many places, gold coins were stocked. The candidates filled their pockets with gold coins while passing through it. They could not dare to dance as the exposure of their theft was imminent. This man is honest, he did not take any coin," the minister explained.

Soul Searching

When one loses one's integrity, he/she is unable to see the truth and think clearly. Then one fails to realise that the *Māyā* has spread its net to catch them. Since they are confused, they are caught in the net and suffer.

"He is the only honest man among them."

43. Association with the Wicked

A king was riding a horse and passing though an unknown village. Suddenly he heard a parrot crying:

"Come! Chase! Catch! Take the horse! Take his jewels!"

The king knew he was among the dacoits. He raced his horse. He was chased but his horse brought him to safety. Then again he heard the call of a parrot:

"Welcome! Welcome King! Come! Sit! O see! A guest! Bring a seat! Bring water!"

The king stopped. He wondered yet he smiled. He was pleased. He came down. It was not difficult to know that it was a hermitage of a great sage.

The sage came out to welcome the king. The king expressed his wonder much before the formalities, "O sage! I have just met another parrot. He cried loudly: 'Come! Chase! Catch! Take the horse! Take his jewels!' But your parrot is different. What is the reason."

In place of the sage, the parrot spoke:

"*Rājan*! We are brothers, the off-spring of the same parents. He was taken away by the dacoits and I came to the sage. It is simply because of our association with different persons and milieu that we are different. He listens to the thieves and murderers and I to the learned and refined words of learned men and sages. That is why we speak differently!"

Soul Searching

The best way to show one's gratitude towards one's master is to follow him. His association is the greatest gift which can be given to others graciously provided that you are under the best master, the real preceptor and not under a cheat.

"*Rājan*! We are brothers, the off-spring of the same parents.

44. Time: A Leveller and Settler

Once, Buddha was walking from one town to another with a few of his followers. This was during the early days when he delivered many discourses everyday. While they were travelling, they passed a lake. They stopped there and Buddha told his disciple who seemed to be a little disturbed.

"I am thirsty. Do get me some water from the lake."

The disciple walked up to the lake. When he reached there, he noticed a bullock cart entering into it and crossing through the lake. As a result, the water became very muddy, very turbid. The disciple thought, 'How can I give this muddy water to Buddha to drink!'

So he came back and told Buddha, "The water in the lake is very muddy. I don't think it is fit to drink."

After about half an hour, again Buddha asked the same disciple to go back to the lake and get him some water to drink. The disciple obediently went back to the lake.

This time too he found that the lake was muddy. He returned and informed Buddha about the same. After sometime, again Buddha asked the same disciple to go back. The disciple reached the lake to find the lake absolutely clean with pure water in it. The mud had settled down and the water above it looked crystal clear. So he collected some water in a pot and brought it to Buddha.

Buddha looked at the water, and then he looked up at the disciple and said, "See what you did to make the water clean. You left it as it was, and the mud settled down on its own. So you got clear water. Your mind is also like that. When it is disturbed, just let it be. Give it a little time. It will settle on its own. You don't have to put in any effort to calm it down. It will happen. It is effortless."

The disciple understood and became claim and peaceful.

> **Soul Searching**
>
> Mind creates modifications. These mental modifications keep a person restless. The tranquility is restored if one stops further creation of disturbing modifications.

"See what you did to make the water clean."

45. The Safest Place

A man was staying with a saint with the idea that the place of a saint is the safest place and death will not dare to come near him. While living with the saint, he had also become pious. But one day, a *Yama Duta*, the messenger of death came there. He was surprised to see that man there. By the surprise look on his face, the man was convinced that he would die soon. He asked, "Why have you come here?"

"I have come to take away the saint." The reply came instantly.

"But the saint has been doing wholesome deeds for quite a long time," the man voiced his doubts.

"What of that! Each one has to die at the designated time and place," the *Yama Duta* gave a straightforward reply.

"Why did you look surprised to see me?" At last, he put the question that worried him.

"It surprised me to see you here with the saint. I shall come to take you tomorrow," he said and went inside.

The man ran away from there fast and travelled with whatever means he could get. He wanted to go as far away as possible. He thought that the messenger of death will look for him at the place of the saint.

He came to a lonely place and hid himself in the basement of a new tower under construction and disguised as a worker. Only after a few hours, the *Yama Duta* came.

He asked, "How did you know that I am here."

"I had the orders to pick you up from here that is why I was surprised to see you there with the saint as I had no idea how you will reach here in less than a day," he explained further.

Soul Searching

Where one feels fully secure, can be the least secure place. It can well be his/ her place of death designed by destiny and earned by *prārabdha karma.* There is no safe place where one won't die. Only good deeds, throughout the life, ensure the death to be the last. For a man with good deeds, there will be no further birth or death.

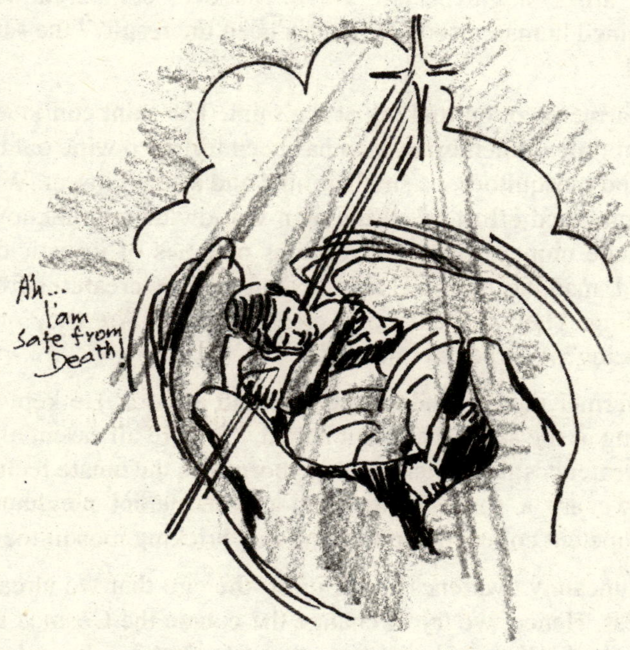

The man was staying with a saint with the idea that the place of a saint is the safest place.

46. Different and Unique

A saint came to a village. He was very old and soft-spoken. People liked him and came to him to listen to his teachings.

The third day, there came a vibrant youthful farmer – laborious and competent. When the discourse was over, he asked the saint, "I want to check the flow of our Dhanauti River so that the farmers can irrigate their crops throughout the year. How can I do it?"

"You are a single person. Have you ever compared with combined human effort? What has been the result?" the saint asked.

The farmer kept on looking at the saint. The saint continued, "From time immemorial, man has been trying to wipe out the rats and mosquitoes – a small animal and a small insect. With the combined effort of all the men worldwide and unknown but huge money spent and millions of tones of insecticides spread, man has not been able to stop the tiny creatures from breeding. They still exist and create menace. Are they only menacing? Are they not needed?"

The farmer neither understood nor said a word. He kept on looking at the saint. The saint added, "We are all essential to the greater cosmic system. We are born with the innate feeling that we are a shade better than our intolerant neighbour, incompetent colleague or nibbling rats pricking mosquitoes.

This uncanny awareness adds up to the ego that we already possess. Hence, we try to change the course the Cosmos has prescribed. We must discover the role that we have been assigned and the role that we can play the best for making life better and more refined. We must realise that every individual, without an exception, is endowed with individual characteristics and hence is different and unique. The river is more useful when it flows throughout the year. To try to check the flow of energy is selfishness and blunder."

Soul Searching

Changing the ways of Nature and natural elements and objects may not yield the expected result.

47. Imaginary Wealth and Fear

Gopal Bhatt lived next door to a poor couple who had the habit of day-dreaming.

One day the husband said to his wife, "If I had some money I would buy a few cows."

"Then we would have a lot of milk," said his wife. "I could make plenty of butter and ghee and we could send some milk to my sister too."

"Send milk to your sister!" exclaimed her husband. "How dare you suggest such a thing!"

"But we would have milk to spare," said his wife.

"We'll sell it!" said her husband. "I don't want anymore talk on the subject and to make sure you don't carry milk to her when I'm away, I'm going to break every pot in the house!" And picking up the four or five pots they had, smashed them on the floor.

Gopal Bhatt, who was passing by at that time, asked him as to why he was breaking the pots? When he learnt the reason, he picked up a stick and started beating the air with it.

"What are you doing?" asked his neighbour, puzzled.

"Driving away your cows!" said Gopal. "They've eaten the cucumbers in my garden."

"Eaten you cucumbers!" exclaimed the other man, indignantly. "But you don't even have a garden!"

"I'm going to have one soon," said Gopal, "and I'm going to grow cucumbers in it." And he began hitting out with the stick again.

The neighbours finally realised that Bhatt was trying to show them, how foolish it was to live in a world of make-believe! They felt ashamed of themselves.

Soul Searching

The world is a roller coaster ride. It is in a constant churn. It is a mix of the pairs of opposite, and definitely unpredictable. Yet the structures are constructed with the mix. One can compare it with the churning of the upper (outer) layer of curd (self). If churned well, one can get both – butter and healthy buttermilk.

48. Rice vs Gold

A beggar saw a king coming. He was extremely excited that the king would pass through his hut. He could not control his excitement. Every moment the king was coming closer, he was losing his composure, not because he was about to see the king at his place but because the king was known to part with expensive jewels and huge sums of money when moved by compassion.

When the king's chariot was exactly at the beggar's hut, a kindly man started filling his begging bowl with uncooked rice. Pushing the man aside, he ran on to the road carrying his bowl and shouting praises of the king and the royal family.

The chariot stopped and the king beckoned to the beggar.

"Who are you?" he asked.

"One of the most unfortunate of your subjects," said the beggar. "Poverty sits on my doorstep and follows me about like a dog's tail. I haven't eaten since yesterday afternoon!"

"Have you nothing for your king except a tale of woe?" said the ruler, putting out his hand. "Give me something."

The beggar, astonished, carefully picked up five grains of rice from his bowl and laid them on the king's outstretched palm.

The king drove away. The beggar's disappointment was great. He raved and ranted and cursed the king again and again for his miserliness. Gradually, he calmed down when all his known curses were repeated many times. Then, he went on his rounds.

When he returned home in the evening, he found a bag of rice on the floor.

"Some generous soul has been here," he thought and took out a handful of rice from the bag. To his astonishment, there was a small piece of gold in it. He realised, then, that the bag had been sent by the king. He emptied the rice on the floor, feeling sure there would be more gold pieces in it, and he was right. He found five gold pieces, one for each grain of rice he had given to the king.

"It is not the king who has been miserly," thought the man sadly. "If I had been generous and given him the whole bowl of rice, I would have been a rich man today."

Soul Searching

In trying hard to know others, one forgets to know oneself. At the spur of the moment one does such things because of the compulsion of his nature and character which force one to repent later.

49. Inner Nature

A sage was taking bath in a river. Suddenly, he saw a drowning scorpion. Out of pity, he picked the scorpion up on his palm. The scorpion at once stung him. He shook his hand out of pain. The scorpion fell in the water again. He again picked it up and again he was stung. The third time he was able to move a few steps towards the bank. But it stung again and fell down.

The sage tried again and again but the result was the same. Now, he was closer to the bank. Another person who was taking bath in the river said to the sage, "O Sage! Don't try to take it out. It will sting you every time you pick it up. It is its nature. It should be killed. Leave it in the water to die. Howsoever hard you will try, it will not change its nature."

Without turning towards the speaker, the sage picked it up again and threw it towards the bank, and said:

"This tiny insect will not change its nature. If humanity is better than animal nature then why should I change my inner nature which is pity and compassion?"

Eventually, the sage succeeded in throwing the scorpion on to the safe ground.

Soul Searching

Humanity is better than animal instinct; kindness is better than cruelty; virtue is better than vice; love is better than hate. We all know it yet we foster the negative qualities.

50. Detached Couple

It is an incident that occurred in the 18th century. After completing his studies, Pt. Shri Rāmanāth Tarka Siddhānta had established his hermitage in the Vidyā Kendra of the then Bengāl. He lived there with his wife as a sage. He had neither accepted stipend from any king nor would ask for anything from anyone.

One day, his wife informed him that there were only two fistfuls of rice in the house and asked, "What should I cook?"

He said nothing. He came out and sat among his students with a book to teach. When he was called for dinner, he found a bit of cooked rice and leaves. He ate and asked, "*Bhadre*! Which green leaves did you cook? They were delicious."

"When you were going out, you looked at the tamarind tree. I have cooked its leaves." She answered.

"I had no idea that tamarind leaves are so tasty." The husband reiterated and added, "Then we don't have to worry about our food."

King Shiva Chandra had heard of his reputation and financial crisis. One day, he went there with the sole intention to help the couple. After the preliminaries, he asked, "O learned teacher! Is there anything that you need?"

"I have completed the book and I don't need anything." His reply was simple.

"I am not talking of *Tarka Shāstra*. I'm talking about domestic need." The king clarified.

"Now, that is not my responsibility. You can ask the house mistress." The reply remained simple.

The king went inside and repeated the question to his wife. She gave a poetic and symbolic reply:

"O king! My hut needs nothing. My clothes have not torn up so much, so they are not to be replaced; the water pot is not broken and till the bangles are in my hands then I have everything in my husband."

The king bowed low and touched the feet of the lady with his crowned head. He was blessed.

Soul Searching

The soul cannot be perceived by material means. One can't definitely define the role of knowledge in understanding the soul. On the spiritual path, the knowledge gained would lead the knower to ultimate peace.

Spiritual Quadruplets

One

We have a body with systems,
organs and a living spirit within;

The body is alive, moves and acts for
the Prāna, life element, is in,

We need a body healthy and active
and a spirited spirit spiritual;

For fruition, prosperity, to bloom with
boughs, flowers, leaves green.

Two

One must foster well and take care of
the two in manner proper;

Their needs are different, opposite, one
to cover, the other discover;

Provide food fresh, healthier, and
ideas moral and benevolent;

Exquisite balance is to be maintained
for ascending steadily higher.

Three

Body is the infrastructure while spirit
is the prudent Proctor;

One is the ship essential, the other is
the sailor, the navigator;

One can't be sacrificed for the other,
as the twins make the whole;

Body needs a soul to be alive, the spirit
needs a body to prosper.

Four

Out of the four common pursuits,
for progress and elevation;

Two, *Artha* and *Kāma* are for the body,
physical attainments;

The other two, *Dharma* and *Moksha*,
are for the soul, the spirit,

To perform pious deeds and strengthen
the claim for salvation.

Five

They get infinite prosperity that live in
harmony with *Prakriti*, the Nature;

Strive hard, incessantly to become sublime,
with steady steps, feature;

They listen to conscience and sincerely
follow its pious, intuitive dictates;

And maintain a balance in ethical earning
and wise, frugal expenditure.

Six

Real prosperity is both the
spiritual and material richness;

To be larger, higher, and to possess
greater scope, wideness;

To feel the importance and need of
all living and non-living;

To exhibit for all: love, sympathy,
compassion and kindness.

– From Spiritual Quadruplets